Nathan
Llewellyn

Year 1.

First published in 1996 by Sapling,
an imprint of Boxtree Ltd, Broadwall House,
21 Broadwall, London SE1 9PL
Copyright © Geoffrey Planer, 1996

10 9 8 7 6 5 4 3 2 1

Reproduction by SX Composing DTP
Printed and bound in Great Britain by Cambus Litho Ltd.

ISBN: 0 7522 2300 3

A CIP catalogue entry for this book
is available from the British Library.

MOUSE TALES

The Princess who Picked her Nose

Geoffrey Planer

sapling

For Nina
(who doesn't)

'And whose turn is it tonight then?'
asked Mr Tail, closing the front door.
365 mice jumped around him.
'Ollie hurt his paw today ...' said Sophie,
'... so we said it could be his go for the story.'
Mr Tail took off his coat and hung it
on the peg by the door.
Ollie tried to climb up Mr Tail's leg.
Simon shouted. Sophie tugged his paw.
'Ollie it is,' said Mr Tail as he firmly
removed Simon from his trousers.
Mr Tail blew Mrs Tail a kiss, chose a
book from the shelf, put his cardigan on
inside out and sat down in the chair
on top of Sophie's biscuit.
'Now, now! Quiet please kids or you
will never find out why the Princess who
lives at the end of the road had nearly
no friends,' said Mr Tail.

Another Night,
Another Mouse,
Another Tale . . .

The Princess who Picked her Nose

There was once a beautiful Princess who was not only perfect to look at but was clever as well; and nice; and kind. But she had one fault.

Although she could
dance divinely,

tie her own
shoe laces,

play the
trumpet

and ride a bicycle ...
she did have one
terrible fault.

Although
she knew
what seven
eights were,

although
she could
peel grapes
with a knife,

although she
could make
a noise like
a monkey
laughing ...
she had
one fault.

She would keep picking her nose.

Her mother,
the Queen,
didn't know
what to do.
She tried
telling
her off;

she tried blowing her nose with
tissues; she tried giving the Princess
a hanky with a 'P' embroidered on it,
but nothing worked. The Princess
just kept on picking her nose.

The Queen asked the King to have a quiet word with her, but that didn't work either. The Princess kept right on picking her nose.

She picked
it at home.

She picked
it at school.

She picked it
in the back
of the car.

She picked
it at night.

She picked it when the King
and Queen took her out visiting.
She picked it when the Royal
Nanny took her to the shops.

The Princess didn't mind
when everyone stared,

but the King, the Queen and the
whole Royal Household were –
well – frightfully embarrassed.

As she grew older, the Princess went
to lots of parties where she met lots of
Princes. She would dance with them,

they would tell jokes, she would laugh
and everything would be fine until, ...
... until she started to pick her nose.

'Yich!' would
say the Prince.
Or sometimes,
'Errrchh!'

Or even, 'Zerrrrrrch!'

The Princess knew
it was rude to pick
her nose, but she
had been doing it
for so long now
that she found it
impossible to stop.

One day the Princess went to a party at a new palace. All the usual Princes and Princesses were there; and they played all their favourite games and danced all their favourite dances. And of course, as usual, no one really wanted to dance with The Princess Who Picked Her Nose.

Now, in the corner of the room stood a new Prince who nobody had seen before. The Princess went over to talk to him.

They talked and talked.
Then they laughed and laughed.

Then the music started
and she asked him to dance.
Round and round they went.

After they'd danced and danced,
they had to stop because they
were tired and thirsty.

The Princess asked the Prince to fetch
her a glass of fizzy water. While he
was gone, she said to herself:

I must not pick my nose;
I must not pick my nose;
I must not pick my nose;
I must not pick my nose;
I must not ...

She looked across the room. She saw the Prince. She stared. She stared again. There he was, standing in a corner, where he thought no one could see him. And do you know what he was doing?

PICKING HIS NOSE!

Of course the Princess and the new Prince
became the best of friends from then on.
They played together every day, they
went on holiday together every summer

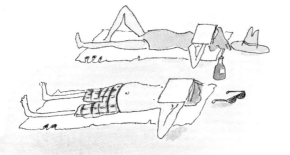

and years later they were married.

And later on, after that, they had five
lovely children, who were beautiful and
perfect in every way, and could sing
lullabies, knit scarves, whistle, do
crosswords and much more.

However, they all had one bad fault.

They would keep picking their ...

... but that's another tale.

'What did they keep picking?' asked Ollie.

'Their noses, silly,' answered Sophie.

'My paws won't really reach my nose,' said Simon, sadly.

'Just as well,' said Mr Tail. 'And now it's bedtime for all Tails,' and he lifted Ollie up onto his shoulders.

'Up the stairs go the ... Simon stop picking your nose!' said Mr Tail as he saw him hiding in the corner of the room.

'I'm not,' said Simon. 'I'm trying an experiment to see if my paw's long enough to reach my nose to scratch it.'

'And I'll try an experiment too ...' but Simon had stopped his experiment and was up the stairs and into bed before Mr Tail could even finish.

Small Tales,
Tall Tales,
Bedtime -
for All Tails